5A

DATE DUE

SEP 17 198

SEP 20 1986

OCT - 6 198

OCT 24 1986

FEB - 3 1987

UUN - 2 1987

AUG - 6 1987

AUG 22 1987

DEC 15 1987

AUG 23 1988

DEC 12 198

APR - 5 1989

JUN 2 9 1989

JUL 2 0 1989

EB 2 8 1990

APR 4 1990

JUL 1 8 1990

G 4 1990

J* CLA
Clardy, Andrea,
Dusty was my friend>< with loss
rdb01633261

1701 92001 73895 2

WITHDRAWN
SALINA PUBLIC LIBRARY

D1366103

J* Cla   6/86

Clardy, Andrea.

Dusty was my friend

Markings noted

SALINA PUBLIC LIBRARY
SALINA, KANSAS
JUVENILE DEPT.

SALINA PUBLIC LIBRARY
SALINA, KANSAS
JUVENILE DEPT.

Dusty Was My Friend

Coming to Terms with Loss

by Andrea Fleck Clardy

Illustrated by Eleanor Alexander

 HUMAN SCIENCES PRESS, INC.
72 FIFTH AVENUE
NEW YORK, N.Y. 10011

Copyright © 1984 by Human Sciences Press, Inc.
72 Fifth Avenue
New York, N.Y. 10011
All rights reserved.
Printed in the United States of America
   3456789 987654321

Library of Congress Cataloging in Publication Data
Clardy, Andrea, 1943-
   Dusty was my friend.

   Summary: Eight-year old Benjamin remembers his
friend Dusty, who was killed in a car accident, and tries to
understand his own feelings about losing a friend in this way.
   [1. Death—Fiction. 2. Friendship—Fiction]
I. Alexander, Eleanor, ill. II. Title.
PZ7C52945Du 1984   [Fic]   83-6203
ISBN 0-89885-141-6

SALINA PUBLIC LIBRARY
SALINA, KAN
JUVENILE DEPT.

dedicated to the memory of
Dustin Lowell Berger

My name is Benjamin and I am eight years old. I used to have a friend named Dusty. In a way I still do, but in a way I don't because he is dead.

Dusty had straight hair and a gap between his front teeth. He was two years older than me, the same age as my brother Peter. We all had violin lessons with the same teacher. Dusty would talk with me while our violins were being tuned and he would laugh whenever I acted funny. He liked me and he was my friend, even though he was my brother's age.

Dusty was killed in a car accident last year. He was coming home from visiting his grandparents for Christmas when the accident happened.

Dusty was killed right away. The rest of the people in his family were hurt very badly, but they all got better after a long time.

We came home from vacation without even knowing about Dusty. The first day after vacation, Peter was in school and one of his friends whispered, "Hey, did you hear that Dusty was in an accident and he got killed?"

"You're out of your mind,"
              Peter said.

He couldn't imagine that
Dusty was dead. He didn't even worry about it. He just went on with his math so that he would be done in time to draw some airplanes. My brother draws terriffic airplanes like Spitfires and C-47 transports whenever he has free time.

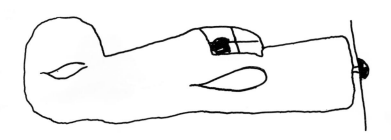

When we got home from school, Mom told us she had some very sad news. Then she told us how Dusty had died. His Dad was driving along the highway when pieces of lumber started falling off the truck in front of their car. Dusty's Dad had to swerve all over the place because of the lumber. Then the truck stopped and Dusty's car ran into it. Some boards from the back of the truck smashed through the windshield. Dusty was thrown off the back seat where he was sitting and he was killed.

It's hard to believe someone is dead when you didn't see anything happen. The only way I could think of Dusty was alive. When I could finally imagine that he wasn't, his dying didn't seem fair.

"Why did Dusty get killed?" I asked my Mom. She didn't know.

"I wish I could explain it to you," she said, "but I can't. This is one of those things that doesn't make any sense to me either."

"But how come it had to be Dusty?"

"It didn't have to be," Peter told me. "It just was."

"Tell me again about the accident," I said to Mom, and she did.

"Is the driver of the truck going to be punished?" I asked my Mom.

"He will probably have to pay a fine because the lumber got loose. And he might lose his driver's license," she said, "because you're not supposed to stop all of a sudden on a highway."

"I think they should put him in jail," I said, "for the rest of his life."

"That's a goofy idea," Peter said.

Mom said, "Think how upset the truck driver must feel. Maybe he's already being punished enough." But his being upset did not help Dusty, so I still thought they should put him in jail.

After that, we couldn't think of anything else to say so we had some hot chocolate.

Later, Peter and I got to thinking. We tried to remember just what we had been doing the day of the accident. We had visited our grandparents during Christmas vacation, the same way Dusty had. The afternoon Dusty was killed, we had been playing down by the beach because our grandparents live near the ocean.

Peter figured out the day and the time. He says that we were building sand castles when Dusty's car crashed. That seems weird to me whenever I think about it. We didn't even know.

The day after we came home and found out, Mom went down to the newspaper office and bought a copy of the newspaper that told about the accident while we were out of town. There was a picture of Dusty. We decided it was probably his school picture. His hair was slicked down and he was wearing a tie so he looked more grown up, but he was smiling his same old smile that showed the space between his front teeth.

For a long time, I thought about Dusty. I couldn't think about him all at once, so I'd think about him little by little. Sometimes I would get so sad my stomach hurt. I don't see why Dusty had to die. My Dad's aunt died, but she was pretty old. And when my gerbil died, I didn't even cry. Dusty was different.

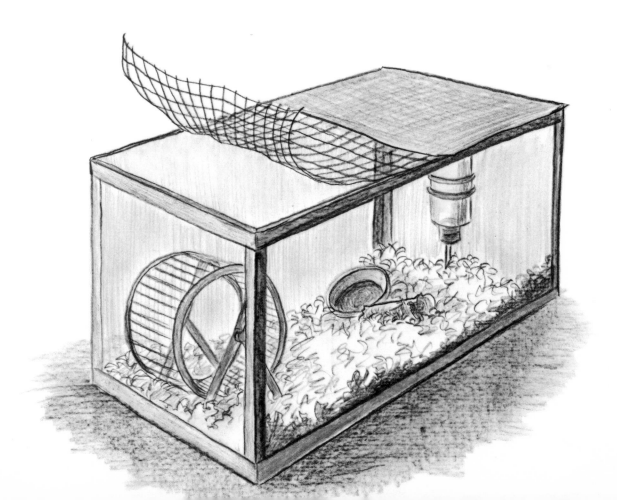

Sometimes thinking about Dusty made me feel scared. I don't want to die. I want to get to be a grown-up, so I'm taller than my Dad, and I can be a deep sea diver or a veterinarian and stay up late at night. My Dad says I shouldn't worry because children almost always grow up safely. But I still do.

Sometimes I'd start crying about something like my best friend Joseph not being home when I wanted him to come and play, or having corn for dinner when my Mom knows I like peas or celery better and it's Peter who likes corn.

We'd end up talking about Dusty lots of times. Then I would feel a little better. We talked about how Dusty would always say "Hi!" to me, even if he was with other big kids. We went to a play at the high school once and Dusty was there and when he saw us, he stood right up and waved.

Dusty knew a lot of knock-knock jokes and he taught me some I can still tell. He played the violin really well and he was nice about it.

I remember that sometimes when I am practicing.

Then I had an idea. I said to Mom, "I want to write Dusty a letter."
She looked at me for a long time and she pushed back my hair where it
falls into my eyes.

"You can't do that," she said.
"Yes, I can."

"Why don't you write a letter to his family.
They would like that."

"I don't know what to say to his family.
Dusty is who I want to write to. And I can
do it myself."

"But Dusty is dead," Mom said.
"He couldn't read it."

"I know that." Of course I
knew that.

I went and found a paper and a pen and I wrote the letter very neatly. It said: "Dear Dusty, I'm sorry that you died. I love you. Benjamin."

Then I didn't know what to do with the letter. I wanted to put it on Dusty's grave. I think a letter would be nicer than flowers. But he is buried far away, where the accident happened in Nebraska.

Maybe someday I'll go there. I'd like to. I have the letter in my secret treasure drawer in case I ever do. Otherwise, I'll just keep it.

When we have violin practice for the whole group, our teacher sometimes says, "Is everybody here?"

"No. Dusty is missing," I always tell her.

It has been a long time now since Dusty died. I still feel like he's missing. But I don't get scared and shy anymore when I think about him.

Whenever I see a cemetery, I wonder about Dusty. Of all the people who have died, he is the one that I care about. I think of him when I see someone who has a space between his front teeth or when I hear the knock-knock jokes he taught me.

I think of him when the violin group plays "Variation on Long, Long Ago" because that was his favorite piece. I think he matters more to me now than he did when he was alive.

Dusty was my friend and I am glad that he was.